Evil Queen Tut and the Great Ant Pyramids

For Judith, and for the real Zack,
with love—D.G.

THE ZACK FILES™

Evil Queen Tut and the Great Ant Pyramids

By Dan Greenburg

Illustrated by Jack E. Davis

GROSSET & DUNLAP • NEW YORK

I'd like to thank my editor
Jane O'Connor who makes the process
of writing and revising so much fun,
and without whom
these books would not exist.

I also want to thank Catherine Daly,
Laura Driscoll, and Emily Neye
for their terrific ideas.

Text copyright © 1999 by Dan Greenburg. Illustrations copyright © 1999 by Jack E. Davis. All rights reserved. Published by Grosset & Dunlap, a division of Penguin Young Readers Group, 345 Hudson Street, New York, NY 10014. GROSSET & DUNLAP and THE ZACK FILES are trademarks of Penguin Group (USA) Inc. Published simultaneously in Canada. Printed in the U.S.A.

Library of Congress Cataloging-in-Publication Data

Greenburg, Dan.
    Evil Queen Tut and the great ant pyramids / by Dan Greenburg , illustrated by Jack E. Davis.
        p.   cm. – (The Zack files ; 16)
    Summary: While on a class picnic in Central Park, ten-year-old Zack gets a chance to study ants close up and personal when he uses way too much of a classmate's diet powder and shrinks to their size.
    [1. Ants Fiction.] I. Davis, Jack E. II. Title. III. Series: Greenburg, Dan. Zack files ; 16.
    PZ7.G8278Ev 1999
    [Fic]–DC21   99-19859
                                                                                                       CIP

ISBN 0-448-41876-2   19 20

Chapter 1

I happen to have a thing about bugs. I mean, they creep me out. But one day I shrank down to the size of a bug. And I hung out with them in the park. That kind of experience always makes you change your mind about things.

OK, I think I might be going too fast for you here. Probably what I should do first is tell you who I am and junk like that.

So here's what you need to know:

• My name is Zack.

- I go to the Horace Hyde-White School for Boys in New York City.
- I'm ten and a half.
- My folks are divorced, which is a drag.

I spend half my time with each. I wasn't with either one of them when this bug thing began, though.

Here's how it happened.

We were having a class picnic in Central Park. Our science teacher, Mrs. Coleman-Levin, gave us all these huge magnifying glasses. We were supposed to crawl around and look at nature up close.

My best friend, Spencer Sharp, was there. He's the smartest kid in the class. Maybe the smartest kid in the whole school. Vernon Manteuffel was there, too. He's the richest kid in the school. He never lets you forget it. Vernon is kind of fat. He also sweats a lot. And when he's mad at you, he sits on you. He is not my favorite person. But you could probably tell that.

Andrew Clancy came along, too. He's this really tall kid who's always trying to top me. Whatever I do, he's always done it before or better. There were maybe fifteen other kids from my class. But I don't feel like listing all their names right now.

Mrs. Coleman-Levin told us to start using our magnifying glasses. Vernon began poking around in the grass with his.

"Ooh, anthills!" said Vernon. I went over to look at them through my magnifying glass. But before I could check them out, Vernon started to stomp on them. I stopped him in mid-stomp.

"What are you doing?" asked Vernon angrily.

"Don't stomp on those things," I said.

"Why not?"

"Because. The ants probably went to a

lot of trouble to build those hills," I said. "I may not be that crazy about bugs. But they have rights, too."

Spencer came over to the anthills. "Did you know that most ants are females? All the workers are, anyway. And they have a queen, who's a whole lot bigger than the workers."

"Who cares?" said Vernon. "Bugs are bugs. And they deserve to be stomped."

Spencer bent over the hills and looked at them through his magnifying glass.

"That's strange," said Spencer. "These anthills are not the usual shape."

I bent down and took a peek, too. "They kind of look like pyramids," I said. "Why is that?" I figured if anybody knew the answer to that, it would be Spencer.

"I don't know," said Spencer. "But they're different from any I've ever seen."

"Lunch!" yelled Mrs. Coleman-Levin. We raced over and spread out blankets.

Mrs. Coleman-Levin had brought a big basket with all sorts of food. Peanut butter and jelly sandwiches. Plain peanut butter sandwiches. Plain jelly sandwiches. Plain bread sandwiches. And lemonade. For dessert she'd promised us a big surprise.

Spencer and I were sure the surprise was going to be Len & Larry's ice cream. That's our favorite. Once we actually won a contest to think up a new flavor for Len & Larry's. Our flavor was Cashew Cashew Gesundheit. But that's another story.

When we finished our sandwiches, Mrs. Coleman-Levin opened up a big plastic jar.

"Class," she said, "here's your surprise dessert. Chocolate-covered ants!" Mrs. Coleman-Levin had a sly smile on her face.

"Oh, right," said Vernon.

"She's not kidding," said Spencer.

Mrs. Coleman-Levin nodded. "In some countries, they're a real treat."

Everybody started making gagging and barfing sounds. Mrs. Coleman-Levin kept right on smiling. Mrs. Coleman-Levin is nice. But she's definitely strange. She wears work boots all the time, even to dress-up parties. And on weekends she works in the morgue, cutting up dead bodies.

"I am not about to eat any chocolate-covered ants," I said.

"Chocolate-covered ants are nothing," said Andrew. "I once ate chocolate-covered cockroaches."

"Well, you don't know what you're missing," said Mrs. Coleman-Levin, popping some into her mouth. "They happen to be very tasty."

Fortunately, Mrs. Coleman-Levin had brought along dessert for normal people, too. Blueberries. I love blueberries, but only if they have lots of sugar on them.

"Mrs. Coleman-Levin, do you happen to have any sugar?" I asked.

"I'm sorry, Zack, I don't," she said. "But why don't you sprinkle a few of these chocolate-covered—"

"Thanks just the same," I said.

Then I noticed a plastic bag on the blanket. In it were small packets of sugar. The kind they give you in coffee shops. I took a couple of packets, and poured one over my blueberries and one into my lemonade.

The sugar tasted a little weird. I was almost done with my lemonade when Vernon saw the empty packets.

"Zack!" he cried. "Did you use any of the packets I left lying here?"

"Just two," I said. "Why?"

"That wasn't sugar, you dork!" said Vernon. "That was Shrink-Away."

"What the heck is Shrink-Away?"

"A diet powder that my mother bought for me. It was really, really expensive. She's going to be *furious* at you for taking it. She's going to make you pay me back, too."

"I'm sorry," I said. "I thought it was sugar."

"Well, I bet it makes you sick," said Vernon nastily. "You're only supposed to take a pinch of it at a time. You used two whole packets, you dork. That's a two-month supply!"

As a matter of fact, I *was* starting to feel kind of sick. I thought I might puke. But I didn't want Vernon to know. I didn't want to give him the satisfaction.

Vernon studied my face.

"So how are you feeling, Zack?" he asked.

"Great," I said. "Perfect. I've never felt better in my whole life."

Then I ran into the bushes. I was sure I was going to puke my guts out.

Chapter 2

I didn't puke. But I felt really weird. My whole body was tingling. And my clothes suddenly seemed a little loose. I mean, my pants felt like they were a size too big. Like they might fall down. The legs slopped down over my feet.

The sleeves of my shirt were too long, also. The cuffs were over my hands. I looked like I was wearing my dad's clothes.

I looked around. And then I noticed something else that was strange. The bushes and trees on all sides of me seemed to be growing. What was going on here?

And then it hit me: My clothes weren't getting bigger. *I was getting smaller!* A lot smaller. I was shrinking fast. Like a pat of butter in a hot frying pan.

Before I knew it, I was no more than a foot high. I couldn't believe it. A minute ago I was a normal-sized boy. Now I was the size of a chihuahua. And I was still shrinking!

I stood in the middle of a pile of clothes that had once fit me. I felt like a circus tent had collapsed on top of me! I lost one sneaker. And I was sinking into the other one. *Fast.* I put both of my feet inside it.

There was a sudden noise in the bushes. I looked in the direction of the noise and got the shock of my life.

A tiger was creeping slowly through the bushes. Its belly was low to the ground. And it was headed straight for me!

Chapter 3

A tiger? What the heck was a *tiger* doing in the middle of Central Park?

Maybe this was a dream. I was going to wake up any second, so it didn't matter what I did. I could yell at the tiger if I wanted to. On the other hand, this just might *not* be a dream. In which case yelling at the tiger would be stupid. Really stupid.

As it crept closer, I realized something. It wasn't a tiger at all. It was a cat! A common cat. I love cats. Well, I *used* to love cats, when I was more than six inches tall.

The cat crept right up to the top of the sneaker. I was shrinking so fast, I was able to slide down to the toe. I couldn't have been more than four inches long by now. About the size of a mouse, I thought.

I think the cat thought that's what I was, too! It stuck a paw into the sneaker. But it couldn't reach me. Then it pulled its paw back out of the sneaker and walked away.

That was some close call! I was shaking pretty badly. By now I'd figured out that my shrinking had something to do with Vernon's stupid diet powder.

I didn't know what to do. But one thing was sure. If I stayed in that sneaker much longer, I'd be too small to ever climb out of it. Besides, it was really stinky in there.

I stood up as tall as I could. I jumped as high as I could. I'm a pretty good basket-ball player. But I couldn't even reach the top of the sneaker to pull myself out.

So I grabbed the laces inside the sneaker and started pulling myself up. Hand over hand. When I got to the top, I peeked out. No cat in sight. I swung a leg over the top of the sneaker and pulled myself out.

The sneaker had grown a lot bigger. Which meant I had grown a lot smaller. I slid down the front of the sneaker. I was twice as big as the lace holes. In other words, I was about as big as a bug. My bare foot could easily fit through the holes.

Then it hit me. My foot wasn't the only thing that was bare around here. I was no longer wearing clothes. I was stark naked in the middle of Central Park!

And then I saw it. An ant. About the size I was. Spencer said most ants are females. I quickly covered up my private parts.

"Hello there," said a pleasant voice. It was the ant. "Why are you holding your hands like that?" she asked.

"Because I'm not wearing clothes," I said.

"Neither am I," said the ant.

"Yeah, but you're a bug," I said.

"So what are you?"

"A boy," I said.

"No, you're not."

"Am too."

"Boys are big. Boys are like mountains. You're my size. You must be some kind of bug I've never seen before. I saw that cat come after you. So I decided to check."

"You know, I wasn't always this size," I said. "I shrank."

"Oh, right," said the ant. "What's your name?"

"Zack," I said. "What's yours?"

"Nefertiti," said the ant. "But you can call me Nef for short." She rummaged around on the ground. She picked up a bit of leaf and a blade of grass. Then she tied the leaf around my waist with the grass.

"This should make you more comfortable," she said.

Suddenly, two much larger ants appeared. They were about twice the size of Nef. They were pretty scary. They had huge pincers, almost like lobsters' claws. They wore little Egyptian-looking headdresses on their heads.

"Come on, you two!" said one of them.

"Uh-oh," said Nef.

"Who's that?" I asked.

"Guards," said Nef. "We're really in trouble now."

"What kind of trouble could *I* be in?" I asked. "I just got here."

"Come along, slaves!" said a guard.

The giant ants shoved me and Nef.

"Hey, cut that out!" I said.

"Shut up, slave!" said the guard.

"I am not a slave," I said. "I'm a citizen of the United States of America."

"Move!" said the guard.

We didn't have any choice but to go along with the shoving.

"Where are they taking us?" I whispered to Nefertiti.

"Back to the Pyramids," she said.

"The Pyramids are in Egypt," I said.

"Not these," she said.

We traveled for what seemed like miles. It was probably only fifteen feet, though.

I had to crawl over a huge, round piece of metal. It was brownish in color, and it had some bearded guy's face on it. The bearded guy turned out to be Abe Lincoln. The round piece of metal was a penny.

Then we passed by a brown mountain that stank to high heaven. That turned out to be a pile of dog poop. The flies buzzing around it were bigger than I was. They had these huge, bulging eyes. Their buzzing sounded like airplane engines. They kept trying to divebomb me. I think they were worried I wanted to steal their poop.

Just past Dog Poop Mountain we saw them: the Pyramids. Gigantic anthills shaped like the Pyramids in Egypt. Gosh, these had to be the same anthills I had stopped Vernon from stomping on. Thousands of slave ants were carrying blocks of stone up the Pyramids. Only they weren't blocks of stone. They were grains of sand.

"Hey, Nef," I said. "Why are all those ants carrying grains of sand up the Pyramids?"

"Because Tut-ant-khamen orders us to."

"Who the heck is Tut-ant-khamen?"

"Our Pharaoh Queen. She forces us to build them. As monuments to her greatness."

"Some monuments," I said. "Every time it rains, her monuments get washed away."

"Queen Tut doesn't care. She has lots of slaves to rebuild them."

"How come everybody obeys her?"

"We have no choice. She's very big. She's a hundred times as big as we are. You can't disobey somebody that big."

"Shut up!" shouted a guard. "Speaking during work hours is strictly forbidden!"

"Sorry," I said. "By the way, when do we get off work around here?"

"You get off work five minutes after you die."

Wow. And I thought the teachers in my *school* were strict. I was clearly in a lot of trouble. If I couldn't think of a way out of it soon, I might never see my mom or my dad again. They'd be running all over New York, looking for me. And here I'd be, a slave in an Egyptian ant colony.

I had to come up with some kind of a plan, and soon. But what?

Chapter 4

The guards dragged us all the way to Queen Tut's throne and threw us on the floor. The throne was decorated with stuff the ants obviously thought was cool. Tinfoil from gum wrappers. Glitter. Tinsel from old Christmas trees.

"Your Royal Highness," said the bigger of the two guards. "These two have escaped from the workforce. What do you want us to do to them?"

"Chop off their tiny heads!" said a loud, raspy voice.

Queen Tut was the biggest ant I had ever seen. She had on a gold crown and slave ants were fanning her with blades of grass. She leaned down and squinted at us.

"Who are they?" Queen Tut asked.

"Slaves, Your Highness," said the guard. "Runaway slaves."

"Ants?"

"Yes, Your Highness," said the guard.

"I am *not* an ant," I said. "I'm a boy."

"You are not a boy!" roared the guard. "Boys are as big as mountains. Boys are bigger than Her Royal Highness, Queen Tut."

"What?" shouted Queen Tut.

"Sorry, Your Highness," said the guard. "Boys are *almost* as big as Her Royal Highness."

"What?" shouted Queen Tut.

"Sorry," said the guard. "Boys are *nowhere near* as big as Her Royal Highness."

"That's better," said the queen. **"Much**

better. Do you have the Royal Axe to chop off their tiny heads?"

"No, Your Highness. The Royal Axe is not yet back from the Royal Sharpener. The Royal Sharpener is a little backed-up because of the holidays and all."

"Oh, poop," said the queen. **"First Queen Tut runs out of chocolate. Then the Royal Axe isn't here to chop off heads. Nothing is going right today."**

"Excuse me, Your Majesty," I said. "But did you say you ran out of chocolate?"

"A Hershey bar that was supposed to last a year," snapped the queen. **"Queen Tut has eaten it in only a month."**

Suddenly I had a plan. A plan to save our tiny heads from being chopped off.

"Uh, I know where there's more chocolate," I said. "Would you like me to get it?"

"You can get more chocolate?" cried the queen. She seemed delighted, like a little kid. **"Chocolate for Queen Tut? Queen Tut *loves* chocolate! Chocolate is Queen Tut's very favorite food!"**

"If you let us, Your Majesty, Nef and I could leave now," I said. "And bring back chocolate for you in less than an hour."

Nef looked as if she wanted to kiss me.

"Bring back chocolate for Queen Tut and you will be handsomely rewarded!" cried the queen.

"We'll go right now, Your Majesty," I said.

"Then go, already!" she shouted.

I grabbed one of Nef's arms—or maybe it was a leg. And we took off.

It was a long way back to the picnic blankets. I mean, for my old self it would have been only a few steps. But for my new ant-sized self it was miles.

I didn't even know which way to go. So Nef led the way. Ants have really great senses of direction. It's like they have Mobil Oil road maps in their heads or something.

Tiny pebbles in our path seemed like boulders. Little puddles looked like lakes. Weeds looked as big as telephone poles.

"How come you guys have Egyptian names and stuff?" I asked. "Are you copying Egypt or what?"

"No, Egypt copied *us*."

"Excuse me?" I said.

"Zack, ants have been on earth a hundred million years, longer than even the dinosaurs. Egypt has been around for a few thousand years. So who's copying whom?"

"Yeah, I see your point," I said. "So tell me, Nef, do you have a husband? And some cute little ant larvae at home?"

Nefertiti started laughing. I don't know if you've ever seen an ant laugh.

"Hoo hoo!" she cried. "Hoo hoo hoo!"

"What's so funny?" I asked.

"Nobody in our colony has mates, except Queen Tut. Which is fine with me. Because the guys in our colony are real losers."

"In what way?"

"They don't do a thing. They eat, they mate, and then they die. Anything that gets done here gets done by the females."

"Does Queen Tut make all the babies?"

"Yes. She lays the eggs. Hundreds of thousands of eggs every year. She has four thousand children. You can't believe what bedtime is like."

"That sure is a lot of babies."

"It sure is. They are cute at the larval stage, though. You should see those little smiles. You could just eat them up! Some *do* get eaten up, as a matter of fact."

"Really? By whom?"

"Hungry guards."

I didn't know what to say to that. So I didn't say anything.

"The rest of us," Nef went on, "chew up leaves and spit them out. The mold that grows on the chewed-up, spit-out leaves is what we eat. It's yummy."

"I think I'll stick with cheeseburgers."

"OK, if you prefer dead cow topped with spoiled and hardened milk, then suit yourself."

There was no point in arguing. So we traveled on. Suddenly, I heard something. Something big. It was crashing through the brush just behind us.

"Zack!" said Nef. "Run for your life!"

I looked back. Crashing toward us was the ugliest thing I've ever seen. It had a low, flat body. Creepy feelers that were longer than its body. Bulging eyes. Scary jaws. A face you see only in horror movies.

Yikes! A cockroach! A cockroach the size of a schoolbus!

Chapter 5

I was running as fast as my little legs could carry me. Tiny drops of sweat were pouring down my face. I was breathing so hard, I thought my ant-sized lungs would burst.

Nef was running fast, too. Pretty soon, she passed me. That wasn't surprising. I mean, she had four more legs than I did.

I looked back. The cockroach was gaining on me! This was it. This was how I was going to die. Not of old age when I was a hundred, but eaten by a cockroach! My life couldn't end that way. It was too stupid!

I looked back again. The cockroach was almost on top of me!

Then, suddenly, I heard a whooshing noise. Something enormous hit the ground like an earthquake. At the same time, I heard a sickening crunching sound.

A giant foot had come down on top of the cockroach! A giant foot in a giant white sneaker with red stripes on it. Roach guts squirted out all over. Some hit me. Ugh!

"Zack! Are you all right?" called Nef.

"Yeah! That was a close one!"

"Watch out you don't get stepped on yourself!"

I was pretty shaky. I didn't know where that giant foot had come from. Probably one of the guys in my class. Whoever it was had saved my life. But I'd probably never be able to thank him. It made me feel awful. I was still alive. But what good did it do me? I wanted my old life back.

Up ahead of us I saw something fuzzy and blue. It looked about three feet thick. I couldn't see how far it stretched, but it was huge. It looked about the size of a big lake. Then I realized what it was. It was the edge of one of the picnic blankets!

"We made it, Nef! We're at one of the picnic blankets. That jar of chocolate is very close by."

We crept along the edge of the blanket. There was a lot of junk on it. A big brown leather baseball mitt. A big new baseball with giant red stitching. A gigantic green canvas backpack, as tall as a building. And, not far from the backpack, the plastic jar filled with chocolate-covered ants. Hooray!

Resting against the jar was the plastic bag with the Shrink-Away packets. The cause of all my trouble! But I realized something. If we climbed to the top of the bag of Shrink-Away, I'd be able to get inside the jar.

Wait a minute! Suddenly I realized something else. The bag of Shrink-Away! My tiny brain had a big idea. A very big idea.

"Tell me, Nef," I said. "What would happen if Queen Tut weren't so big?"

"What do you mean?"

"I mean, what if Queen Tut suddenly started...shrinking? What if she shrank down to our size? Or even smaller? Would anybody still take orders from her then?"

"No, of course not. But nothing could ever make her shrink like that."

"Maybe there is something," I said. "Do you see the stuff inside this bag?"

"What?"

"Listen. I shrank down to ant size because I ate a lot of this stuff. It's something called Shrink-Away."

"What's Shrink-Away?"

"Diet powder. Very strong stuff. Very expensive. If we bring some back to the royal chamber and feed it to Queen Tut..."

"Then maybe she'd shrink, too?"

"And we'd be rid of her. What do you think?"

"It's worth a try."

All we had to do now was get a few grains out of one of the packets and carry them back, along with some chocolate.

Nef and I tried to scramble into the bag. It was sealed shut. I couldn't pull it open.

"What do we do now?" I asked Nef.

Instead of answering, she chewed a hole in the plastic, and we crawled inside. Cool!

It was hot and sweaty inside the plastic bag. We were standing on a packet of Shrink-Away. Without my asking, Nef chewed a hole in the side of the packet we were standing on.

"Be careful, Nef," I said. "You chew up a tiny bit of one of those grains, you'll get so small I won't even be able to see you."

We lifted out a few grains of Shrink-Away. They were spikey, white, and the size of soccer balls. As we stood looking at the grains, the ground began to shake.

"Uh-oh," said Nef. "We'd better go!"

I carried the grains of Shrink-Away outside and looked around. The shaking had stopped. And then I saw them. Two gigantic feet. Attached to the feet were legs as tall and as big around as the trees in Redwood National Forest. And above the legs, way above them, looming like a mountain in the clouds, was the biggest butt I had ever seen in my entire life!

Suddenly, without warning, it started falling right toward us like an asteroid! We were about to be sat on!

Chapter 6

"Falling butt! Falling butt!" I screamed.

I pushed Nef out of the way just in time. The giant tush missed us by inches. The wind from the landing blew us a couple of yards away. I held onto the Shrink-Away with all my might.

"Whew! Thanks, Zack!" said Nef. "You saved my life!"

That would have been a horrible way to die. Who the heck belonged to the behind that almost killed us? Who else but...Vernon! I recognized his khaki shorts.

I was so mad at him, I wasn't thinking straight. Without stopping to worry about danger, I ran right up and bit him.

I heard a tremendous shout. Like the trumpeting of an elephant. Then a giant hand slapped where I had bitten. He just missed me.

"Well, *that* was stupid," Nef scolded. "You could have gotten killed. Come on, Zack. We'd better get back to the Pyramids."

"Not so fast, Nef," I said. "We've got the Shrink-Away, but we still need the chocolate. What we have to do is stick some chocolate on the Shrink-Away to make her want to eat it."

"Then let's get that chocolate," said Nef. "Now!"

And then I realized the problem. There was chocolate inside the jar, all right. Chocolate covering up dead ants.

"Um," I said. "Nef, this is something that I must do alone. Where I go, Nef, you must not follow."

"Why can't I help you?"

"That is something I can never tell you," I said dramatically.

I mean, how do you tell a friend that her people were the main ingredient in a dessert?

Climbing into the container of chocolate-covered ants was pretty grim. It was worse than I would have imagined. I guess that's what happens when you've become friends with an ant.

I felt like puking again. I tried not to look at the dead ants buried in the chocolate. I broke off a large chunk of ant-free chocolate. And I climbed out of that container as fast as I could go.

Working quickly, Nef and I broke the

chocolate into tiny pieces and smooshed them on the grains of Shrink-Away.

"Now let's get out of here!" I said.

With both of us carrying the chocolate-covered Shrink-Away, we took off for the Pyramids. We had to trick Queen Tut into eating the Shrink-Away. If my plan didn't work, then poor Nef and her family would be slaves for life. So would I, for that matter.

Chapter 7

We returned to the throne room.

"**So you are back,**" said the queen. She giggled. "**And what is it that you hold in your tiny hands?**"

"Chocolate, Your Majesty," I said.

"Shut up, slave!" shouted a guard. "Did anyone tell you to speak?"

"**No, let him speak,**" commanded Queen Tut.

"Speak, slave!" shouted the guard.

"We've brought your chocolate, Your

Majesty," I said. "The finest chocolate candy in the kingdom."

"You will be rewarded," said the queen. **"Handsomely rewarded. Now give the chocolate to Queen Tut."**

Nef and I started to hand the chocolate-covered grains of Shrink-Away to her. The guards snatched them out of our hands. Then *they* handed them to Queen Tut. The queen gobbled them up in a single gulp.

"Good chocolate," she said. **"Semi-sweet, and not too filling."**

"Glad you liked it, Your Majesty," I said.

I watched the pharaoh queen closely. Nothing seemed to be happening to her. Maybe it would take a while. When I ate the Shrink-Away, it didn't work on me right away. No, come to think of it, it did.

"Have you brought any more choco-late?" asked Queen Tut.

"No, Your Highness," said Nef. "That's all we had."

"OK," said the queen. **"Now chop off their tiny heads."**

"What!" I shouted. "You can't do that!"

"Of *course* Queen Tut can do that," she said. **"Queen Tut can do anything she pleases. Queen Tut is the boss!"**

"But you told us we were going to be rewarded!" I cried.

"You *will* be rewarded," she said. **"As a special treat, after they chop off your heads, we will put them on lovely wooden plaques. They will hang on the wall in the Royal Chamber. It is the highest possible honor."**

"You can't chop off our heads!" I shouted. "We brought you chocolate!"

"Take them away," commanded Queen Tut. **"They are becoming tiresome."**

The guards grabbed us roughly and began

to drag us out. Suddenly, we heard a big belch. It had come from the giant ant queen. The guards stopped and looked at her. Nef and I looked, too.

She seemed confused. She seemed dizzy. She seemed kind of sick.

"Queen Tut is feeling a little woozy here," she said. **"Queen Tut is feeling like maybe she's going to whoops. Are you sure that chocolate wasn't spoiled?"**

"That wasn't ordinary chocolate, Fatso," I said. "That was Shrink-Away diet powder."

I don't know why I called her Fatso. Probably because the most she could do to me now was refuse to put my head on a plaque. And I didn't really care about that.

Suddenly, the ant queen shuddered. The guards rushed forward to help her. She fell off her tinfoil throne onto the floor. She kept shuddering. And getting smaller!

"What is happening to Queen Tut?"

she shouted. **"What is happening to Your Royal Highness?"**

She shook like crazy. And she shrank some more.

"Help your Pharaoh!" she screamed to the guards.

"What can we do, Your Highness?"

"Queen Tut doesn't know. But if you cannot help your Pharaoh, then your Pharaoh commands you to chop off your *own* heads. And don't you dare put them on lovely wooden plaques either. Or you'll be sorry!"

The guards didn't know what to do. They just stood there as Queen Tut grew smaller. And smaller. And smaller.

Soon she was only twice as big as us.

"Help me!" she cried in a much smaller voice. "Somebody help me!" Now she was exactly the same size as Nef. Then she was only half that size. And soon we could barely see her at all. She was just a dot on the floor. And then, even the dot disappeared.

"She's gone!" I yelled.

Nef and I hugged each other.

"We're free!" she said.

"No, you're not," said the guard. "We've been ordered to chop off your heads."

"You were also ordered to chop off your *own* heads," said Nef. "Are you going to do that, too?"

The guards looked at each other. Then they shrugged.

"Uh, you do have a point there, slave," said the guard.

"I'm not a slave anymore," said Nef. "And you're not guards anymore. We're all free ants now. We can do whatever we want. Queen Tut is dead!"

The guards looked at each other again.

"Sounds right to *me*," said one of them.

"Hey. Me, too," said the other.

"Well, hope there are no hard feelings," said the other. "You guys take care."

Hundreds of ants who'd heard what happened crowded around the throne.

"Queen Tut is dead!" Nef announced. "We're free ants now." The ants cheered. She turned to me. "And it's all thanks to Zack," she said. "You have saved my people. You must become our new leader."

The ants cheered some more. "Zack for pharaoh!" they shouted. "Zack for pharaoh!"

"Oh, no thanks," I said to the crowd. "I'm not even an ant. If anybody should lead your people, it ought to be Nefertiti."

The crowd went wild. "Nefertiti for pharaoh!" they shouted. "Nefertiti for pharaoh!"

"But I'm not big enough to be a queen," said Nef. "I'm only worker size."

"Eat the royal leaf mold!" yelled one of the ants.

"Well," said Nefertiti, "I suppose I could. But I'd sure have to eat an awful lot of royal leaf mold to get as big as a queen."

Wait. What was this I was hearing? I looked Nef right in the eye.

"Is that how queens grow to be so big?" I asked. "From the mold on chewed-up, spit-out leaves?"

"Well," she said. "It's a special kind of mold. We make it just for queens."

I didn't want to get too worked up. But maybe there was hope for me.

"What do you think would happen to me if *I* ate some of that stuff?" I asked.

"You'd probably throw up," she said.

"Could I try some anyway?"

"Are you serious?"

"I think so," I said. "It may be my only chance to get human-sized again."

Nef went over to a matchbox next to the royal throne. She pulled it open and took out some nasty-looking stuff. She handed it to me.

"This is it?" I asked. "The special mold you feed only to ant queens? The kind that grows on chewed-up, spit-out leaves?"

"Yes," she said.

I sniffed the stuff. It smelled pretty yucky. It smelled pretty moldy. If I ate it, would it make me grow? Or would it make me dead? But what choice did I have?

I wanted to go back to my friends and my family. I missed Spencer and Andrew Clancy. I even missed Vernon...well, almost.

I took a taste of the leaf mold. It was just as awful as I thought it would be. But I kept eating it.

The good news was, it wasn't poison. The bad news was, I was still exactly the same size I was before I ate it.

"I guess it doesn't work on humans," I said sadly.

"I'm sorry, Zack. What will you do now?"

"I don't know," I said. "I think I'll go back to the picnic. Maybe I can find Mrs. Coleman-Levin. Maybe I can climb up inside her ear and talk to her. I remember she once said somebody put a bug in her ear."

"Good-bye, Zack," said Nef. She and all the ants waved lots of arms at me. "My people will never forget what you did for us. We shall build a statue in your honor. You will always have a home with us."

"Good-bye, Nef," I said. And then I took off again into the wilds of Central Park.

Chapter

8

I had never felt so alone. What was going to become of me? How would I ever live as a bug? At least I wasn't hungry. I'd eaten enough leaf mold to last me for days.

I passed by Dog Poop Mountain again, and the huge penny.

But I couldn't find the picnic blankets. Had the class gone home? If they had, there was no way I would ever find them. I sat down on the ground and closed my eyes.

I was thinking very seriously of crying

when I heard something. A creaking noise. Then a popping noise. Then nothing. Then another creaking noise and another popping noise. Then I felt a tingling all over my body. And guess what? My arms started stretching!

I watched in amazement. My arms got to be twice as long as they were before, and then stopped growing. The same thing happened to my legs. And my neck. Then nothing.

I waited. Sure enough, there were more creaking and popping noises. I was growing again! I had now grown right out of my leaf toga. I was stark naked again. I must have been at least a foot tall by now!

I looked around. Yes! About fifty yards ahead of me I saw them. The picnic blankets! Thank heavens!

Just then I had another growth spurt. It happened faster, this time. I searched madly for my clothes. I couldn't find them anywhere. Had somebody stolen them?

Now I was two feet tall. Now three. A huge squirrel ran by and stopped in his tracks. He stared at me. You could tell he was trying to decide whether to take a bite out of me. Then I grew another foot. I growled at the squirrel. He took off.

I was almost back to my normal size! The leaf mold had really worked! And there in the bushes were my clothes! I rushed to put them on. I was just stepping into my pants when I heard a voice behind me.

"Young man, what are you doing in the bushes with your clothes off?"

I turned around. It was Mrs. Coleman-Levin. She had a weird expression on her face.

"Uh, hi, Mrs. Coleman-Levin," I said.

"You haven't answered my question," said Mrs. Coleman-Levin. "I'm waiting."

"Well," I said, "do you want a nice normal answer? Or do you want the truth?"

"The truth."

"OK. The truth is, I ate two packets of Vernon's Shrink-Away, and I shrank to the size of an ant. I didn't fit into my clothes anymore, but this nice ant named Nefertiti made a leaf toga for me. So then I became a slave in an ant colony that was building pyramids for this mean ant queen named Tut-ant-khamen. Did you know that queens are a whole lot bigger than other ants?"

"Yes, about a hundred times as big, in fact," said Mrs. Coleman-Levin.

"Uh, right. So then Nef and I fed this ant queen a few grains of Shrink-Away, covered in chocolate, and she shrank down to nothing. Then Nef gave me some special stuff that they give only to ant queens..."

"Leaf mold," said Mrs. Coleman-Levin.

"Right. It tasted yucky. But then I grew

back to my normal size, and here I am. And that's pretty much what happened."

She looked at me carefully for a moment. I had no idea what she was thinking.

"Well, Zack," said Mrs. Coleman-Levin. "It sounds as if you had a much more interesting picnic in the park than the rest of us. If you like, tomorrow in class you can give a special talk on ants for extra credit. But if I were you, I'd leave out the part about your shrinking and being part of the colony."

"It really happened, though," I said.

"I didn't say it didn't," she answered.

I buttoned up my shirt and walked back to the guys.

"Hey, Zack," said Spencer. "Where have you been?"

"Studying ants," I said.

"You were gone for at least twenty minutes," said Spencer.

"Is that all?" I asked. I was sure I'd been

gone for several hours. But that was probably in ant time.

"You were studying ants for the whole twenty minutes?" asked Andrew. "How come it took that long?"

"Well," I said, "if you want to know the truth, I actually joined an ant colony."

"Oh yeah?" said Andrew. "I joined an ant colony once. It took me only fifteen minutes, though."

Vernon came up, rubbing his waist.

"The trouble with picnics," he said, "is all the darn bugs. Do you know one bit me right on my waist?"

I started to giggle. Then I looked at Vernon's feet. I couldn't believe my eyes.

He was wearing white sneakers. White sneakers with red stripes! The same sneakers that had squashed the giant cockroach!

Vernon Manteuffel was the kid who saved my life!

Chapter 9

When I got home from the picnic, Dad asked me how it had gone. I said fine.

"Anything exciting happen?" he asked.

"Not really," I said. Later I'd tell him about my adventures. But right now I was a little tired from carrying grains of sand and being chased by cockroaches and all.

"You know something, Zack?" said Dad. "I think you're looking taller."

Dad made me stand against the kitchen doorway. He makes pencil marks there to record my height. He'd measured me only a couple of weeks ago. I'd grown an inch and a half from the special leaf mold!

I've gone back many times to the place in the park where we had that picnic. I've taken a magnifying glass and crawled all over the place. But I've never been able to find those pyramid-shaped anthills or Nefertiti's colony.

I know they're out there somewhere, though. And wherever they are, there's a tiny, ant-sized statue of yours truly.

Hey, top *that* one if you can, Andrew Clancy!

What else happens to Zack?
Find out in
Yikes! Grandma's a Teenager

Early Sunday morning I was awakened by a scream. I jumped out of bed. I dashed out of my bedroom.

Standing in front of the full-length mirror on the bathroom door was Grandma Leah. Except it wasn't Grandma Leah. It was a teenaged version of Grandma Leah. The only way I knew it was Grandma was that she was wearing Grandma's fuzzy pink slippers, her fluffy pink robe...

..."Grandma, is that really you?" I asked. I sounded like Little Red Riding Hood.